Big Tooth!

by **Jenny Jinks**

illustrated by
Daniel Limon

Fred went zooming along.

"What is it, Fred?" said Tad.

"It's Big Tooth!" said Fred.

And he hid in the reeds.

Tad swam off in a panic.

"What is it?" said Pop.

"It's Big Tooth!" said Tad.

And he hid in the reeds.

Pop swam off in a panic.

"What is it?" said Chip.

"It's Big Tooth!" said Pop.

Then he hid in the reeds.

Chip shot off. "Big Tooth?"

And he hid in the reeds too.

All the fish hid.

Then a big fish swam up.

"Big Tooth!"

"Shhhh," said Fred.

"He will not see us."

"Eat you?" said Big Tooth.
"No! Fred and I are playing
hide and seek."

"You got me," said Fred.

"Now it is my turn to seek."

Quiz

1. Fred went _____ along.
a) jumping
b) zooming
c) fishing

2. Where do the fish hide?
a) In the reeds
b) In a rock
c) In a shell

3. Why are the fish in a panic?
a) Small Fish is coming
b) It's a race
c) Big Tooth is coming

4. What does Big Tooth say when he finds the fish?

a) BOO!

b) BAM!

c) Surprise!

5. What game were they playing?

a) Chase

b) Cops and robbers

c) Hide and seek

Book Bands for Guided Reading

The Institute of Education book banding system is a scale of colours that reflects the various levels of reading difficulty. The bands are assigned by taking into account the content, the language style, the layout and phonics. Word, phrase and sentence level work is also taken into consideration.

Maverick Early Readers are a bright, attractive range of books covering the pink to white bands. All of these books have been book banded for guided reading to the industry standard and edited by a leading educational consultant.

To view the whole Maverick Readers scheme, visit our website at

www.maverickearlyreaders.com

Or scan the QR code above to view our scheme instantly!

Quiz Answers: 1b, 2a, 3c, 4a, 5c